Usborne

Stories
of
Dragons

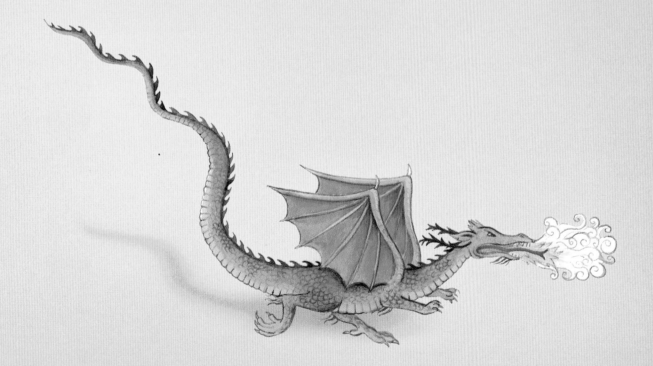

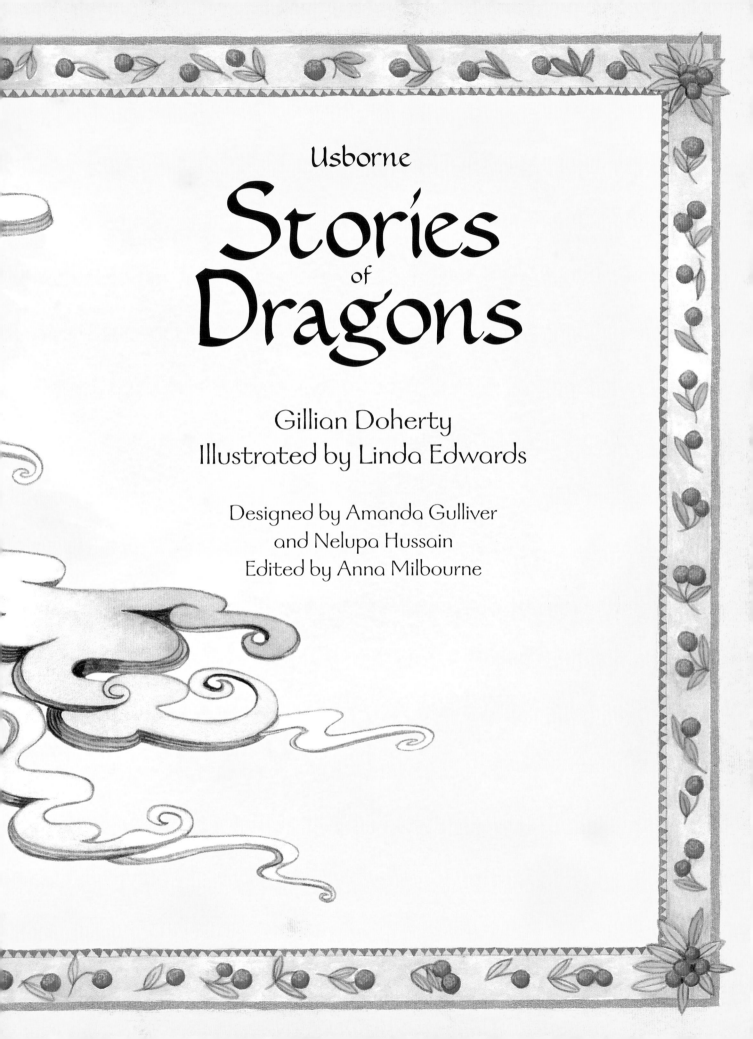

Usborne

Stories
of
Dragons

Gillian Doherty
Illustrated by Linda Edwards

Designed by Amanda Gulliver
and Nelupa Hussain
Edited by Anna Milbourne

Contents

6   The Dragon Princess
17   The dragon's treasure
24   George and the dragon
30   A banquet for dragons
36   The dragon and his grandmother
46   The lace dragon

54   Rustam's faithful horse

60   The thirsty dragon

66   The big fish

71   Jack and the dragaman

80   The dancing dragon

89   Mysterious Melusine

The Dragon Princess

Deep beneath the Eastern Sea was the magical underwater kingdom of the Dragon King. For hundreds of years, he had ruled the waves, turning the tides and keeping the sharks in order, but all that was nothing compared to the challenge that faced him now. With his daughter's eighteenth birthday fast approaching, it was time to find her a husband.

All the most handsome young princes from the undersea world were brought to the palace. They wore their finest silk robes and brought extravagant gifts. But the Dragon Princess was not impressed. As the dolphins nudged each prince forward, she noticed that not a single one of them was able to look her father in the eye.

Again and again she shook her head
and turned her face away.

"My dear daughter," said the Dragon
King in despair, "we've searched high and low
for a suitable husband for you, but you don't
seem to like any of them. What sort of husband
would you like?"

The princess searched deep in her heart
for the answer. "I just want a man who
is honest and brave," she sighed.
"These princes may be rich,
but they're all too afraid
to look at you. What
sort of husbands
would they make?"

The Dragon King loved his daughter dearly, so he sent all his most trusted advisors to search beyond his kingdom for a husband to suit her. Marshal Crab searched the beaches, Prime Minister Turtle checked all the ships and General Eel inspected the rivers.

Only General Eel managed to find someone answering the princess's description. "I've found just the man," he said triumphantly. "His name is Ayer and he lives on the river bend with his brother. He's very, very poor, but he's known far and wide for his honesty and bravery."

The Dragon Princess clapped her hands in delight. "He sounds like the perfect husband for me!" she exclaimed.

But the Dragon King frowned. "I really don't think he's good enough," he muttered. "He's a land lover and as poor as a sea slug. And, anyway, how can we be sure he's honest and brave?"

The princess tossed her head and stormed to her room. For days, she refused to eat or to speak to anyone. Seeing her so upset made the sea creatures unhappy too. The whales sang sorrowful songs, the clams hid away inside their shells and the puffer fish were terribly deflated.

"I've got an idea," said Marshal Crab at last. "Why don't we test this young man to see how honest and brave he is? If he passes, then you can be sure he will make a good husband."

The Dragon King liked the idea, so that night Marshal Crab appeared to Ayer in a dream. "There's a beautiful girl waiting on the riverbank," he said. "Go and ask her to marry you."

Ayer woke up, his heart pounding with excitement. He shook his brother, Ahda, and told him about his dream.

"What nonsense!" said Ahda. "Go back to sleep." But, secretly, Ahda believed his brother and wanted the girl for himself. He waited until Ayer was fast asleep; then he crept outside and raced down to the river.

When Ayer woke up again, his brother's bed was empty. "He must have gone to the river," thought Ayer, and hurried after him.

It was a beautiful moonlit night, with fireflies flitting across the river like dancing stars. Ayer found his brother crouching in the long grass. He knelt down beside him and followed his gaze to the opposite bank, where a beautiful girl was sitting. Ayer knew she was the one. Leaping to his feet, he burst out eagerly, "Will you marry me?"

"No! Marry me," shouted Ahda, pushing Ayer out of his way.

"Which of you is more honest and brave?" asked the Dragon Princess, for it was she.

"I am," they replied in unison.

"Then you must prove it," she said. "Whoever brings me the pearl that shines by night will be my husband."

"But where will we find it?" asked Ahda.

The Dragon Princess took two combs from her hair and tossed them across the river. "You must go to the kingdom of the Dragon King, in the Eastern Sea," she said. "These magic combs will part the waves so that you may enter."

The two brothers didn't even know where the Eastern Sea was, but Ahda borrowed a horse and galloped towards the rising sun and Ayer followed on foot.

After several days, Ahda arrived at a village that had been destroyed by a flood. The villagers were all gathered on a hillside, discussing what to do.

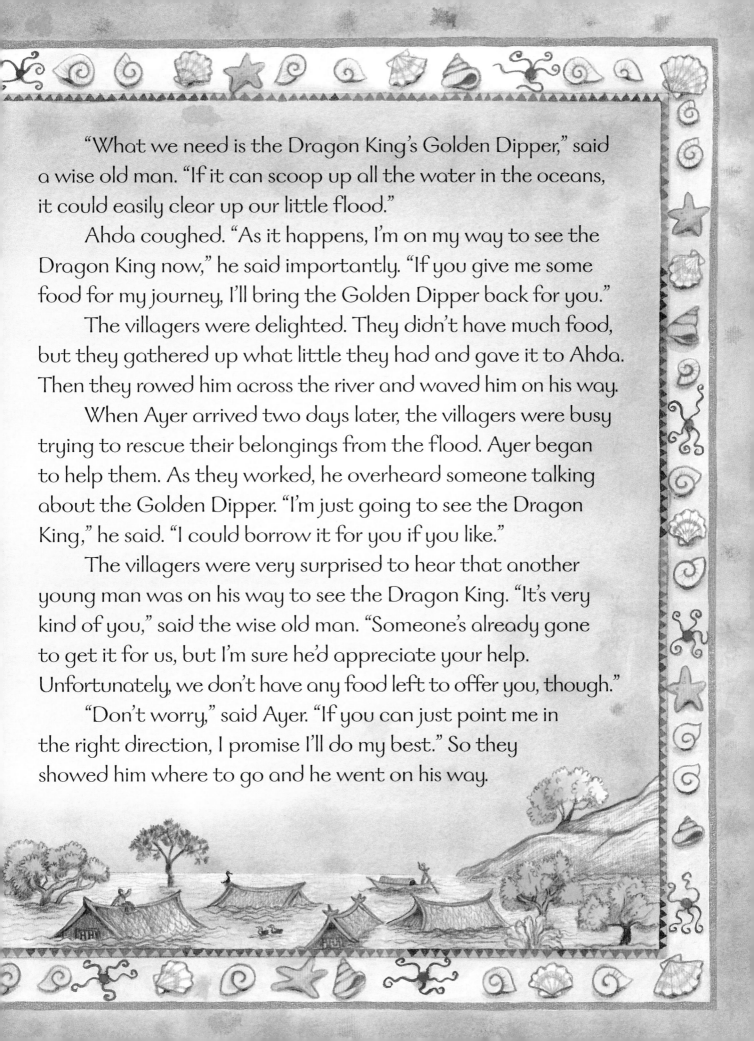

"What we need is the Dragon King's Golden Dipper," said a wise old man. "If it can scoop up all the water in the oceans, it could easily clear up our little flood."

Ahda coughed. "As it happens, I'm on my way to see the Dragon King now," he said importantly. "If you give me some food for my journey, I'll bring the Golden Dipper back for you."

The villagers were delighted. They didn't have much food, but they gathered up what little they had and gave it to Ahda. Then they rowed him across the river and waved him on his way.

When Ayer arrived two days later, the villagers were busy trying to rescue their belongings from the flood. Ayer began to help them. As they worked, he overheard someone talking about the Golden Dipper. "I'm just going to see the Dragon King," he said. "I could borrow it for you if you like."

The villagers were very surprised to hear that another young man was on his way to see the Dragon King. "It's very kind of you," said the wise old man. "Someone's already gone to get it for us, but I'm sure he'd appreciate your help. Unfortunately, we don't have any food left to offer you, though."

"Don't worry," said Ayer. "If you can just point me in the right direction, I promise I'll do my best." So they showed him where to go and he went on his way.

When Ayer reached the Eastern Sea, he found Ahda staring anxiously at the waves. They were rushing onto the seashore like a herd of charging horses.

"I thought I'd better wait in case you needed some help," said Ahda. Yet he hung back and allowed Ayer to go first.

Ayer took out the comb the princess had given him and plunged it into the water. The waves reared up and up until they towered above him and his brother, leaving a narrow path to the depths of the sea.

Ayer stepped forward. The vast walls of water threatened to sweep him away at any moment, but he was not afraid. Not wanting to be left behind, Ahda grabbed hold of his brother's shirt.

Eventually, they arrived at a huge golden gate where two swordfish and hundreds of soldierfish were on guard. "We're here to see the Dragon King," announced Ayer. Ahda poked his head from behind him and nodded in nervous agreement.

"You may enter," said one of the swordfish, lowering its weapon. "He's expecting you."

A little pilot fish bustled out to meet them. "Follow me," it said briskly.

As the gate swung open, the brothers gazed up in wonder. The palace was dazzlingly beautiful, with magnificent towers that glistened in the underwater gloom.

The two brothers followed the little fish through the palace doors and into a cavernous hall. At the opposite end, sitting on a golden throne, was the Dragon King. The brothers bowed before him. Then, looking him steadily in the eye, Ayer explained why they had come.

When he had finished, the Dragon King nodded, and he showed them to a room at the back of the hall. "This is my treasury," he said. "You are welcome to take whatever you want, but you may take only one item each."

Ahda's eyes gleamed greedily when he saw the glittering array of treasures. But Ayer's heart was heavy. "If I may take only one thing, I must keep my promise," he thought, and he looked for the Golden Dipper. Ahda didn't give it a second thought.

One treasure in the room shone much brighter than all the rest: a beautiful, shimmering pearl. He pounced on it at once.

Ayer picked up the Golden Dipper. "Thank you, Your Majesty," he said to the Dragon King.

"You're very welcome," he replied, and beckoned the little pilot fish over to show them the way out.

Ahda stayed close to Ayer until they reached the seashore. Then he sprang onto his horse and raced away. Soon, he reached the flooded village, where the villagers rushed to greet him. "Did you find the Golden Dipper?" asked the wise old man.

"The Dragon King wouldn't give it to me," lied Ahda, and he kicked his horse and galloped on.

Two days later, Ayer reached the village. "Come quickly," he called. "I've brought the Golden Dipper." When the villagers saw it, they all cheered and hurried down to the water with him.

Ayer plunged the Golden Dipper into the flood. With the first scoop, the water rushed out of the houses; with the second scoop, it drained from the fields; and with the third scoop, every last drop disappeared from the little village.

"How can we ever thank you?" said the wise old man. Then something in the mud caught his eye. It was an oyster. He picked it up and opened it. Inside, there was a jet-black pearl. The old man held it out to Ayer. "Please accept this as a sign of our gratitude," he said solemnly.

"You're very kind," said Ayer, tucking the pearl into his pocket. Then he said goodbye and set off home.

Meanwhile, Ahda was almost at the river bend. When he saw the Dragon Princess waiting there, he waved his pearl in the air.

"I've brought the pearl that shines by night," he cried jubilantly. "Now you must be my wife."

"Not so quickly," she said. "We must wait until tonight to see whether it is the right pearl."

As the afternoon light faded, the pearl became duller and duller, and by the time the moon appeared, it was as drab as a stone. Ahda was furious. He hurled the pearl to the ground and stamped on it.

He was still sulking when Ayer arrived on foot two days later. "I'm very sorry," Ayer said to the Dragon Princess. "I wasn't able to bring back your special pearl, but someone gave me this one." He reached into his pocket and took out the black pearl, feeling a little ashamed of such a feeble offering.

The Dragon Princess took it from him. "Let's wait until tonight to see whether it's the right one," she said.

As night fell, the pearl grew brighter and brighter. It was no longer black and dull; it was like a miniature moon, shining with silvery light. In fact, the moon herself felt so outshone that she hid behind a cloud.

The Dragon Princess tossed the pearl lightly into the air. There was a flash of light so bright that Ayer had to close his eyes. When he opened them, a glorious palace stood before them. The Dragon Princess took Ayer by the hand and smiled at him happily. She had found her brave, honest husband at last.

The dragon's treasure

Late one afternoon, a god named Loki was walking beside a river when he saw an otter lazing on the riverbank. Loki's eyes lit up. "That would make a tasty snack," he thought. He picked up a large rock and hurled it at the otter, hitting it right on the head.

Loki hurried over to claim his prize, but instead of an otter he found a dwarf lying dead in the long grass. He recognized him straight away. It was Otto, a young dwarf who could transform himself into an otter whenever he liked. Every day, Otto went fishing in the river, in his otter form of course. But not any more. Loki had killed him.

Filled with horror, Loki picked up the dwarf and carried him to his father's house. When Otto's father, Reidmar, saw his son, he was overwhelmed with grief. He sank to his knees and beat the ground with his fists. "My poor boy," he wailed.

"I'm sorry," said Loki. "It was a mistake."

"What's the use of being sorry?" cried Regin, Otto's younger brother. "That won't bring him back."

Loki shrugged helplessly. "What can I do?" he said.

Otto's eldest brother, Fafnir, stepped forward. "There is something you could do," he said, with a greedy glint in his eye. "Our brother deserves a decent burial.

If you bring us his weight in gold, it will go some way to repairing the wrong you have done."

Loki nodded. Although he didn't have the gold himself, he knew where he could find it. Further up the river was a waterfall where a dwarf called Andvari kept his store of treasure. It was guarded by a huge pike, but Loki wasn't afraid of a mere fish, even if it was bigger than him. All he had to do was catch it and the rest would be easy.

The very next morning, he took a net and went to find the waterfall. It was a strange spot for fishing, but he settled himself down and lowered the net into the water. Hour after hour passed by and nothing happened. Then, just as Loki was ready to give up, he felt the net grow heavy.

He hauled it to the surface and came face to face with the monstrous fish. It snapped at him with its sharp teeth and writhed around, trying desperately to escape. Keeping his fingers out of the way, Loki held onto the net tightly and pulled as hard as he could.

Suddenly, the fish catapulted out of the water and landed on top of him. As he grabbed it, the thrashing tail seemed to kick at him and the shiny fins became hairy arms. Instead of a slippery fish, he was clutching a wriggling and rather grumpy dwarf. "My, my!" exclaimed Loki. "What have we here?"

"Never you mind," spluttered a dripping Andvari. "Just let me go."

Loki laughed. "In good time, my little friend," he said. "But, first, you must give me all your gold."

"What gold?" muttered Andvari warily.

"I think you know what I mean," said Loki .

"All right, all right," said Andvari reluctantly, "but you'll have to let me get it."

"Very well," said Loki. He opened the net and Andvari dived back into the water.

A few minutes later, the dwarf emerged holding a few pouches of gold. "And the rest," said Loki impatiently.

Andvari frowned and dived in again. This time when he surfaced, Loki was standing waiting with his hands on his hips. "Give me a chance," grumbled Andvari, and down he went again.

"That's everything," panted the dwarf as he came up for the third time. Clambering onto the riverbank, he threw down the final batch of treasure.

Loki smiled and shook Andvari's hand. As he did, he saw a glimmer of gold. His grip tightened. "I said *all* your gold," he growled. Andvari's eyes flashed dangerously. "It's my ring," he hissed, snatching his hand away. This was no ordinary ring; it was a magical ring that brought wealth to whoever owned it, and Andvari was loath to give it up.

"It makes no difference," said Loki. "Unless you give it to me, you're my prisoner, so either way it's mine."

The dwarf's face clouded over. He wrenched the ring from his finger and flung it at Loki. "Have it then," he said bitterly, "but I curse whoever owns it."

As Loki slipped it on, he felt a rush of dizzy excitement. Hardly able to think straight, he loaded the gold into a cart and returned to Reidmar's house.

Fafnir took control immediately and began weighing out the treasure. "There isn't enough," he declared as he placed the last piece of gold upon the scales.

"What do you mean?" said Loki. "Of course there is."

"I'll be the judge of that," snapped Fafnir. "I asked for my brother's weight in gold and that's what I meant." Then he saw the ring on Loki's finger. "That ring should balance the scales," he growled.

Reidmar saw the murderous look in Fafnir's eyes and stepped in front of him. "I'll take that," he said calmly.

Loki shrugged and handed it over.

That night, Fafnir dreamed of the ring. When he woke up, he could think of nothing else. Burning with desire, he went to see his father. "That ring must be valuable," he said. "Why don't you let me take care of it?"

When Reidmar started to shake his head, Fafnir flew out of control. He made a grab for his father's pocket, but Reidmar knocked his hand away roughly. "Give it to me," roared Fafnir, drawing his sword.

"No," Reidmar cried. "I've already seen what it does to you. It's too dangerous."

"If you won't give it up, I'll have to kill you," said Fafnir. Without a moment's hesitation, he drew his sword and plunged it into his father's stomach. Reidmar's eyes filled with pain, and he slumped to the ground.

With trembling hands, Fafnir reached into Reidmar's pocket and took out the ring. As he put it on, he felt an overwhelming sense of exhilaration.

Fafnir took the gold and hid himself in a cave in the hills, far away from anywhere. Afraid that someone would try to steal the ring and his treasure, he never slept or even went outside. All day, every day, all he did was count his gold and stroke the precious ring.

Soon, Fafnir became so ill-tempered that his eyes grew mean and narrow. His skin turned dry and scaly from lack of sunlight, and his teeth grew bigger as hunger took hold of him. His legs shrank too, until he could hardly walk at all, so he dropped onto all fours instead.

Little by little, day by day, Fafnir changed, until one day his transformation was complete. He was no longer a greedy dwarf; he had turned into a dragon.

22

George and the dragon

"Enough is enough," declared the king. "It's time to fight back."
The crowd cheered and charged down to the lake. But, a few
moments later, they came charging back with a ferocious
dragon hot on their heels. "Close the gate," they yelled,
tumbling into the town.

They were just in time. As the gate slammed shut, the dragon
crashed against it. It was hungry and very, very angry. "Send out
the sheep!" shouted the king. The guards opened the gate
just a little and pushed out two frightened sheep.

The dragon snatched them up one after the other.
With two loud gulps, it swallowed them whole, and then
thundered away down the hill.

Everyone breathed a huge sigh of relief,
except the king's chief advisor, who was looking
rather worried. "Ahem," he coughed nervously.
"I'm afraid that was the last of the sheep."

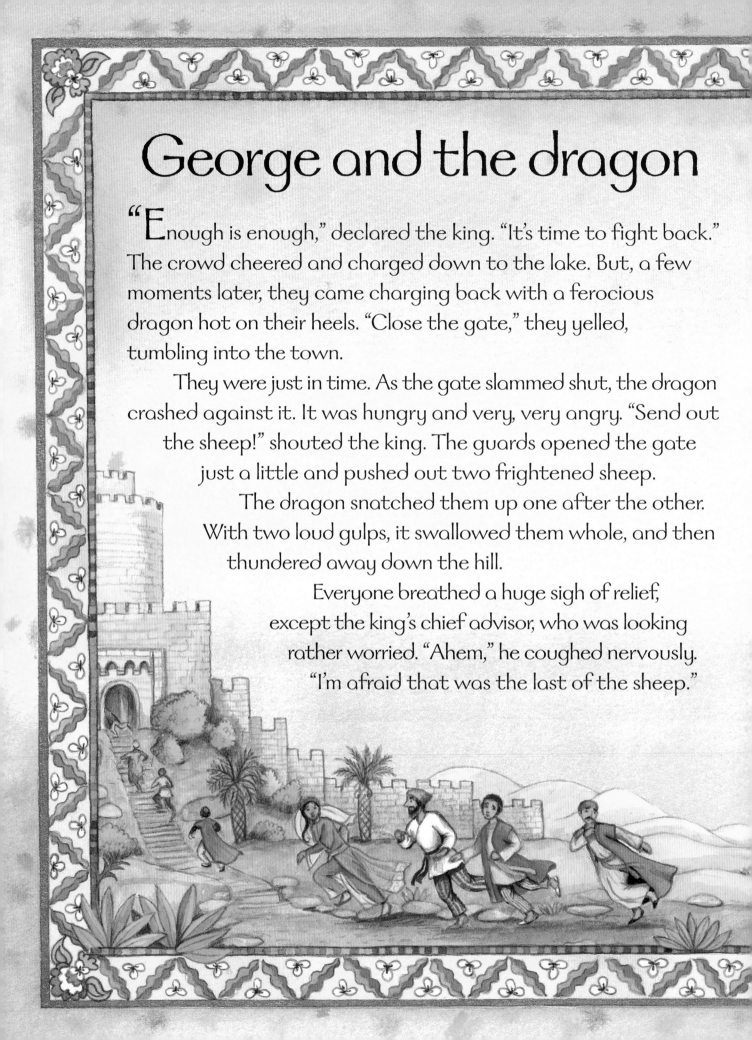

There was a silence. "You all know what that means," said the king sadly. "There's nothing left for the dragon to eat. Tomorrow, everyone's names will be put into a pot, and the person whose name is pulled out must be fed to the dragon."

The very next day that was just what happened, and the day after, and the day after that. As long as the dragon had enough to eat, it left the rest of them alone.

Then, one day, the princess's name was pulled out of the pot. The king turned pale. "Not my lovely daughter," he begged. "Take all my gold and silver and even my entire kingdom, but please don't take my daughter."

His people were furious. "This was your idea," they shouted. "We've given up our children to feed that monster. Why should you be any different?"

The king was heartbroken, but he knew they were right. "Forgive me," he said, throwing his arms around the princess.

Eventually, the king tore himself away, and collapsed on the ground, weeping. His people wept with him, for in spite of their anger they all loved the princess too.

The princess walked slowly through the crowd and made her way to the lake where the dragon lived. There, she sat down all alone and waited, with tears trickling down her face.

After a little while, she heard the sound of hooves, and a handsome knight rode up to her. "What's wrong?" he asked. "Is there something I can do to help?"

"If you want to help yourself, you'd better leave now," sobbed the princess.

The knight didn't move. "My name is George," he said gently, "and I'm not going anywhere until you tell me why you're crying."

So the princess began to tell him all about the dragon. But, before she had finished, she was interrupted by a terrible roar. The dragon reared up out of the lake and ran at them, its eyes blazing.

George lowered his lance and charged. When the lance struck the dragon's chest, it splintered into a thousand tiny pieces, for the dragon's heart was harder than any stone.

As the dragon spun around in fury, its whip-like tail knocked George off his horse. Quickly, he sprang to his feet and drew his sword. With all of his strength, he lunged at the dragon, but it hardly even seemed to notice.

26

The dragon spread out its wings and took to the air.
It circled, then swooped down, shooting flames from its mouth.
It was almost upon them when George saw his chance. Beneath
its wings was soft, pale flesh. Quickly, he thrust his sword
upwards. The dragon let out a deafening shriek and tumbled
to the ground.

George rushed over to it. It was lying very still, but it
was alive. He turned to the princess. "Give me your sash,"
he said. "Let's take the dragon back with us, so everyone can
see that it won't hurt them any more."

George tied the sash around the dragon's neck and tugged
on it gently. With a groan, the beast lumbered to its feet. The
princess gasped and shrank back, but the dragon hung its head
meekly, and she saw, to her surprise, that it was no longer a threat.

Together, George and the princess led the dragon into
the town. Everyone screamed and ran inside. "Don't worry,"
called George. "We've tamed it. Come and see."

A few people peered around their doors. "He's right!"
exclaimed one man. "It's like a pet dog."

"Whoever would have thought it?" said the man's wife, shaking her head.

Soon, the whole town was out in the streets, clapping and cheering. The king heard the noise and came to see what was happening. "Oh, happiest of days," he cried when he saw the princess. Sweeping her up in his arms, he hugged her until she could hardly breathe.

At last, he turned to George. "Brave knight," he said, "you have saved us all. Name your reward."

"Thank you," replied George. "Please don't think me rude, but I already have all that I need. I must leave now – there are others who need my help." And a moment later he was gone.

But the dragon stayed on in the town, living in the castle gardens. From then on, the only people who were afraid of it were the king's enemies, so it made the perfect guard-dragon.

A banquet for dragons

Taru was a mighty storm-god, but he seemed far from powerful after his battle with the dragon Illuyanka. The creature had wounded him badly and his kingdom lay devastated, its green hills scorched brown by the dragon's fiery breath.

"I want my daughter. Bring her to me quickly," moaned Taru, as his servants carried him back into the palace.

Taru's daughter, Inara, hurried to his bedside. "Father, you're hurt," she gasped.

"It's nothing," said Taru. He tried to sit up, but a surge of pain forced him to lie down again. "Illuyanka is destroying me," he groaned. "I don't know what to do."

Inara thought for a moment. "I've got an idea," she said, and she bent down and whispered her plan into Taru's ear.

First thing the next morning, Inara dressed up in her finest clothes and hurried down to the cave where Illuyanka lived. "Great Illuyanka," she called, "my father is very badly hurt. He asked me to come here and make peace with you. Please will you and your children join us for a banquet at the palace tonight?"

She heard scuffling and snarling in the cave, but there was no reply. "I do hope you'll come," she continued. "It would mean so much to us."

Still there was no reply, so Inara left Illuyanka to think it over and went back home to prepare a banquet.

To be sure that the food was absolutely perfect, Inara made everything herself. She cooked juicy meats and fresh fish, and baked deliciously soft bread, as well as hundreds and hundreds of cakes and pastries. The servants carried out flagons of wine and barrel upon barrel of beer. Then Inara waited.

As the food was cooking, the most irresistible smells wafted from the palace and drifted over to Illuyanka's cave. His nostrils twitched and his mouth began to water. Although he was rather suspicious of this sudden invitation from his enemy, he had an enormous appetite and the wonderful smells were far too tempting for him to resist.

It wasn't long before Inara heard the dragons' heavy footsteps approaching. Illuyanka burst into the hall followed by a troop of smaller dragons, all exactly like their father.

Inara bowed down low before them. "You are welcome, Illuyanka, and your children too," she said politely. "I'm afraid my father won't be able to join us tonight, but please make yourselves comfortable."

Illuyanka snorted loudly and made straight for the head of the table, where Taru usually sat. His rudeness made Inara grimace, but she bit her lip and said nothing.

The foul creature began gorging himself immediately. He gobbled up the fish and gulped down the wine, tore at the meat and crunched on the bones, cramming food into his immense mouth until it overflowed.

The little dragons clambered all over one another, nipping and scratching to get at the food. Greedily, they snatched up the scraps Illuyanka spat out and guzzled the wine that dribbled from the corners of his mouth.

Every now and then, Illuyanka would belch loudly. The force of the blasts sent the little dragons rolling head over heels, but moments later their slobbering mouths were back again, gaping for more food.

The dragons ate and ate and ate. They ate so much that Inara thought they would burst out of their scales, but still they kept on eating.

When he could eat no more, Illuyanka heaved himself to his feet. Without so much as a thank you, he lurched out of the palace, with his round-bellied children waddling in a line behind him.

Inara slipped out after them and followed as closely as she dared. When the dragons reached their cave, Illuyanka stooped to go first. He got halfway and then he stopped. The entrance was too small, or rather Illuyanka was too big! He growled at his children to give him a push. They prodded and shoved, and he wriggled and squeezed, but it was no good. He was stuck fast.

This was the moment Inara had been waiting for. "Now!" she called.

At once, her father's chariot burst through the clouds. "I may be injured, but I'm not finished yet," shouted Taru. "Now let's see who's in charge." He raised his bow and fired a shower of arrows at the great beast.

Illuyanka's furious bellows echoed around inside the cave as, one after the other, the arrows hit their mark. But there was nothing he could do. After a while, he stopped struggling and became still. Illuyanka was dead.

When the little dragons saw this, they ran for their lives. With every step they took, flowers and plants sprang up behind them, until all of Taru's kingdom was green again. No one found out what became of the little dragons, but they never, ever came back.

The dragon and his grandmother

A great battle was raging on the plains, and brave soldiers on both sides were dropping like flies. "I don't want to die," whined one soldier as a bullet whizzed past his head.

His two friends agreed. "Why don't we run away?" suggested one.

"Because if we run away the king will have us killed for being cowards," said the other.

"Not if he can't find us," replied the first. "We could hide in that cornfield over there."

It seemed like a good idea, so the soldiers waited until no one was looking and scrambled over to the cornfield. Then, making sure they were well hidden, they settled down and waited for the battle to come to an end.

One day passed, and then
another, but still the battle continued.
The soldiers grew hungrier and hungrier.
"We'll starve to death," groaned one,
rubbing his empty tummy.

Just then, there was a gust of wind. They
looked up and saw a dragon hovering above them,
beating his leathery wings. "What have we here?" he said.
"Some *brave* little soldiers hiding from the battle?"

"We're doomed!" wailed the soldiers.

"Oh I don't know about that," said the dragon
thoughtfully. "Perhaps I can help."

They all looked doubtful.

"I could easily carry you out of here," added the dragon.
"In fact, if you come with me, you will live like kings for seven
years, with as much gold as your hearts desire."

"What's the catch?" asked one of the soldiers.

The dragon's eyes glinted. "There is no catch," he said.

"So what happens when the seven years are up?" persisted the soldier.

"Then I will prepare a delicious feast for you," said the dragon. "If you can guess what will be your meat, your spoons and your cups, I'll set you free. But if you can't, you must be my slaves forever."

"I knew it. Why is it that there's *always* a catch?" complained the soldier.

Nevertheless, the thought of all that gold was very tempting and the soldiers didn't have much choice. It wasn't long before they had agreed to the deal. The dragon picked them up in his claws and flew high into the sky, far away from the battling armies.

38

When the dragon eventually set them down, he handed them a whip. "Each time you crack this whip, you will have as much gold as you wish for," he told them. "Enjoy it while it lasts. I'll see you in seven years."

The three soldiers watched until the dragon was out of sight. Then they stared at one another and at the whip. "We might as well give it a try," said the first soldier, and he cracked the whip. A little heap of gold appeared. He cracked it again and a bigger heap appeared beside it.

"Let me have a turn," said the second soldier, grabbing the whip from him. CRACK! Gold rained down around them until they were up to their necks in it.

"We're rich!" squealed the third soldier.

There was so much gold that the soldiers hardly knew what to do with it. They bought suits of velvet and silk, and rode in elegant carriages, but still there was more gold. They ate banquets every night and built magnificent palaces, but still there was more gold. So they set off to explore the world. They rode through deserts on camels, climbed mountains on yaks and sailed the seven seas, but still there was more gold. Of course, the one thing gold couldn't buy was time, and that flew by more quickly than they could ever have imagined.

As the seven years drew to an end, the three soldiers grew more and more miserable. One day, they were sitting under a tree, surrounded by piles of gold, when an old man came up to them. "So much gold and such long faces," he said. "What on earth is the matter?"

When they had told him their story, he nodded. "Your only hope is the dragon's grandmother," he said. "She lives in a little wooden house in the middle of the forest. One of you must go there and ask for her help."

"I'll go," offered the first soldier. "If it wasn't for me, we wouldn't be in this mess."

By the time he found the little house, it was dark. Bravely, he marched up to the door and knocked loudly.

There was no answer, so he went inside. "Hello, dear," came a voice from the corner. The soldier spun around, expecting to be confronted by an enormous she-dragon, but all he saw was a little, white-haired old lady. His face filled with confusion.

"Perhaps you were expecting someone a little bigger?" she chuckled. The soldier nodded.

"And scalier?" she asked. He nodded again.

"Then you must be here about my grandson," she said. "You'd better tell me what's happened."

So the soldier told the story again. When he had finished, the old lady peered over her glasses at him. "Well, a deal's a deal," she said, "but you seem like a nice young man, so I'll see what I can do to help."

Just then, the clock began to chime. "Quickly," cried the old lady. She opened the hatch to the cellar and pushed him through it. "Hide here and don't make a sound," she said.

As the clock struck midnight, the door flew open and the dragon's head poked into the sitting room.

41

The soldier looked through the hatch and watched in amazement as the dragon squeezed his enormous body through the tiny front door.

"Sit down, dear," said the dragon's grandmother. "Supper's ready." As the dragon sat down, the legs of the little stool bowed under his weight. "How was your day?" asked the old lady brightly.

"Nothing special," shrugged the dragon, "but I'm really looking forward to tomorrow."

"Why's that?" asked his grandmother.

"I'm meeting three soldiers, and if they can't answer my questions, they'll become my slaves," said the dragon.

"What sort of questions?" she inquired.

"I'm going to prepare a feast for them," explained the dragon, "and they have to guess what will be their meat, their spoons and their cups."

"Well, how on earth are they supposed to know that?" said the old lady. Down in the cellar, the soldier pricked up his ears.

"That's the point!" said the dragon, looking very pleased with himself. "They'll never guess in a million years." He lowered his voice to a soft growl. "Their meat will be a dogfish from the North Sea, their spoons will be the ribs of a whale and their cups will be horses' hooves.

"It doesn't sound like much of a feast to me," said the old lady. "I'd rather have a nice bowl of soup."

The dragon and his grandmother chatted on into
the night until at last the beast's head began to nod. A few
moments later, he was snoring loudly. The old lady hurried over
and opened the hatch. "Thank you so much," whispered the
soldier, as he climbed out of the cellar.

He hurried back to his friends, who were delighted to see
him, particularly when they heard what he had discovered.

At noon the next day, the three soldiers met the dragon
in the place where he had left them seven years before. "So,
are you ready for your final feast?" said the dragon slyly.

"I don't think anybody mentioned anything about final,"
said the first soldier. "You told us that if we guessed correctly,
you would set us free."

"Yes, of course," snapped the dragon. "Details, details.
So tell me...what will be your meat?"

"That's a tricky one…" said the first soldier, pretending to mull it over. "Could it be a dogfish from the North Sea?"

"Perhaps that was too easy," muttered the dragon. He turned to the second soldier. "What will be your spoons?"

The soldier scratched his head. "Let me think," he said. "If the dogfish is from the sea, perhaps the spoons come from the sea too. Could they be the ribs of a whale?"

A black look crept across the dragon's face. "Now you," he growled at the third soldier. "What will be your cups?"

The third soldier froze. He had forgotten. "I…errr…wait a minute. I'm sure I know the answer."

"You've got exactly one minute," said the dragon, and began to count on his claws. "One, two…" The seconds ticked by. "Eighteen, nineteen, twenty…" Beads of sweat broke out on the soldier's forehead. "Fifty-eight, fifty-nine, si—"

"Hooves!" blurted the soldier. "Our cups will be horses' hooves." He had remembered just in time.

The dragon knew when he was beaten. With a screech of fury, he snatched up the whip and took to the air.

The three soldiers set off back to their palaces, but they were nowhere to be found. All their gold had disappeared too. "That's the last time I ever make a deal with a dragon," grumbled the first soldier, and his friends agreed.

From then on, they had to earn their money, just like everybody else. The funny thing was that, after a while, they even began to enjoy it.

The lace dragon

In a tiny village in the mountains, there lived a beautiful girl known as Sister Lace. Of course, that wasn't her real name, but everyone called her Sister Lace because of the exquisite lace that she wove. She was so skilled that people would come from miles around just to watch her.

Her fingers danced to and fro like butterflies in a summer breeze. She embroidered flowers so lifelike you could almost smell their scent, animals so convincing they looked ready to leap out at you and birds so intricate they nearly sang aloud. Even delicate spiders' webs sparkling in the morning dew looked clumsy beside her work. She wove pretty collars and cuffs, elaborate tablecloths and bedspreads, elegant shawls and veils – anything that anyone asked her to make.

Eventually, word of Sister Lace's talent reached the emperor, who called for his general. "Why haven't I heard of this girl before?" he demanded. "Bring her here at once."

So the general took three soldiers and set off that very day to search for Sister Lace. They rode through the kingdom and over the mountains until they reached her village. "Where is this girl who makes beautiful lace?" asked the general.

The villagers couldn't imagine what the emperor's soldiers might want with Sister Lace, but they showed them where they could find her.

46

Sister Lace was sitting on the porch when the general and his soldiers marched over. "Can I help you?" she said, surprised to have such important visitors.

"You must come with us now," barked the general. "The emperor wants to see you."

Sister Lace shook her head. "This is my home," she said quietly, "and I do not want to see the emperor."

"What?" spluttered the general. "How dare you disobey the emperor's order. Men, seize her!"

The soldiers didn't move. He turned to find them standing in a row and staring, utterly captivated by the movement of Sister Lace's nimble fingers. "Wake up!" he snapped.

The soldiers blinked and looked around in confusion. "I said seize her!" yelled the general.

This time, the soldiers did as they were told, and carried Sister Lace away to the court of the emperor. "Welcome," said the emperor, as they brought her before him. "I hope you like your new home."

"This is not my home," she said defiantly.

"Don't worry. You'll soon get used to it," he said.

Sister Lace bowed her head as if to kiss his hand, but instead she bared her teeth and sank them into it as hard as she could.

"Yooooooooow!" shrieked the emperor, snatching his hand away. His face flushed red with pain and rage. "Take her away and lock her up," he commanded.

The next morning, Sister Lace was brought before the emperor again. "You must stop this silliness," he said firmly. "I've decided to forgive you and make you my wife."

"I'd rather die than marry you," gasped Sister Lace in absolute horror.

"I'm sure that can be arranged," piped up one of his advisors. "You should have her executed for such impudence," he said to the emperor.

"Fool!" yelled the emperor. "After all the trouble I've had to bring her here, is this the advice you give me? It's you who should be executed. Get out of here. Now, has anyone got any better ideas?"

Another advisor crept forward nervously and whispered in the emperor's ear. The emperor nodded in approval and turned to Sister Lace. "I've heard all about the amazing lace you weave," he said. "If you can make me a live rooster out of lace, I'll let you go home. If not, you must stay here with me. You've got seven days."

In her dark prison cell, Sister Lace wept the night away, but when morning came she dried her tears and set to work. Day and night, night and day she worked, not sleeping a wink. She worked so fast that her fingers bled.

By the time the sun's rays streamed through the bars of the window on the seventh morning, Sister Lace had made a beautiful lace rooster. As she picked it up, her fingers smeared the rooster's comb with blood. It wasn't alive, but it looked just like a real rooster.

Sister Lace hung her head sadly. A large tear rolled down her cheek and splashed into the rooster's mouth. To her complete surprise, the bird sprang to life and crowed to welcome the morning.

Suddenly, the cell door flew open and in burst the emperor. When he saw the rooster strutting up and down, he stopped in his tracks. He stared at Sister Lace in amazement. Then a suspicious look crept across his face. "You've cheated!" he exclaimed. "That's not made of lace at all. It's just one of the palace roosters. You'll have to do better than that. I'll give you seven more days. This time, you must make me a partridge. If you can do that, I will allow you to go home."

When the rooster heard the emperor's words, it was so disgusted that it flew at him and scratched his head with its claws. "Poor, poor Sister Lace," it said. "How I hate the emperor." With that, it flapped past the emperor and out of the open door.

The emperor stormed away in a fury, dabbing his bleeding head with his handkerchief.

Sister Lace's eyes filled with tears. It seemed hopeless, but she bowed her head and set to work once more. Day and night, her fingers threaded and twisted, looped and spun. No matter how tired she became, she kept on going, desperately hoping to please the emperor so she could escape.

At last, just as the seventh morning began to dawn, Sister Lace laid down the lace partridge. She stroked the bird softly with her bleeding fingers, leaving a smear of blood on its breast and a pattern of red speckles on its feathers. "Poor little thing," she said gently. "Do you hate this prison too?" As she spoke, a tear trickled from the corner of her eye and splashed into the partridge's mouth. Instantly, the partridge fluttered its wings and began to fly around the room.

At that moment, the emperor arrived. "What's this?" he blustered when he saw the partridge. "That's not what I asked for. I wanted...errr...a dragon. I'll give you one more chance," he said, "but if you can't make me a dragon within seven days you must stay here forever."

On hearing these words, the partridge flew at the emperor and scratched his neck. "Poor, poor Sister Lace," it said. "How I hate the emperor." And, with that, it flew over the emperor's head and out through the door.

With his pride wounded as much as his head and neck, the emperor stomped out of the cell.

Sister Lace was exhausted by now, but you would never have guessed. She worked harder than ever, hoping with all her heart that this time the emperor would allow her to go free.

By the time dawn had turned the sky rosy-pink on the seventh morning, Sister Lace had made a small but exquisitely formed lace dragon. She looked at it and sighed. Blood from her sore fingers had soaked into the lace, turning it fiery red. "It's no use, my little dragon," wept Sister Lace. "The emperor will only go back on his word again. I don't think he'll ever let me go home."

As her tears fell into the dragon's mouth, it gave a little wriggle and burst into life. At that very second, the emperor arrived. When he saw the dragon, he stepped back in alarm, even though it was so small. "That's not a dragon!" he exclaimed. "It's...errr...a snake."

The little red dragon swelled with indignation. It grew and grew until it was bigger than a tiger and then, opening its mouth wide, it shot forth a ball of flames.

Soon, the entire palace was ablaze. The emperor and his advisors ran for their lives, leaving Sister Lace alone with the dragon. "Poor, poor Sister Lace," it said. "Let's get out of here." She climbed onto its back and the dragon swooped out through the prison door and up into the sky. In no time at all, the flaming palace was far behind them. Sister Lace was on her way home.

Rustam's faithful horse

Prince Rustam had been riding all day and he was exhausted. As night fell, he settled down beneath a tree to rest, and before long he was sound asleep.

Rustam's horse, Rakush, was keeping watch nearby. The trees shuddered in the wind, making him restless. His keen ears twitched at every little sound. Suddenly, the wind changed. Rakush's nostrils quivered; he could smell danger in the night air.

A moment later, there was a flash of gold between the trees. In a single powerful leap, a lion sprang onto the horse's back. Screaming with terror, Rakush reared up on his hind legs. Somehow, he managed to fling the lion aside.

It turned around, snarling ferociously. Rakush reared up again, waving his front legs wildly in the air. With deadly force, he brought his hooves crashing down on the lion's head. The life faded from its eyes and it fell to the ground.

Rustam rushed over, his sword at the ready, but he saw immediately that the lion was already dead. "Brave, brave horse, you have saved both our lives," he said, patting Rakush's neck. "But please be careful, my friend. If anything like this happens again, you must wake me up."

The next day, they crossed a vast
expanse of rocky desert. The sun's rays
burned down upon them, and there was no
shade or water anywhere.

Eventually, just as the sun was sinking
down in the sky, they came to a spring. It was a
welcome sight. Desperately thirsty, Rustam fell to his
knees and began to scoop the cool, refreshing water
into his mouth. When he had finished, he lay down
beside the spring and fell fast asleep.

Rakush stepped forward to drink too, but
as he lowered his head, he thought he heard
a noise. He gave a snort of alarm.

Rustam jumped up. "What is it? Where?" he demanded, spinning around to face every direction in turn. There was nothing there. Rustam relaxed. "You silly horse," he said affectionately. "What are you panicking about? The lion's dead. Calm down and let's get some sleep."

Rustam lay down and soon he was snoring away, but Rakush couldn't settle. As the moon drifted in and out of the clouds, the horse peered anxiously into the darkness. Everything was still and silent. Then, suddenly, Rakush saw what had been making the noise. Out of the shadows loomed the unmistakable shape of a dragon. It came closer and closer. Rakush neighed loudly and beat the ground with his hooves. To his astonishment, the dragon vanished.

Rustam sat bolt upright. "What is it? What's going on?" he cried in confusion. Then he saw Rakush prancing nervously from side to side. "What's the matter now?" he groaned.

Rustam searched all around, but he couldn't find anything out of the ordinary.

"You see," he said to Rakush. "There's absolutely nothing to worry about. Now settle down."

Rakush shook his head.

"Look, I need some sleep," said Rustam wearily. "If you can't behave yourself, I'm afraid I'll have to tie you up." He slipped a rope around the horse's neck and tied it to a tree. "Now, don't wake me again," he said firmly.

No sooner was Rustam asleep than Rakush caught sight of the dragon's red eyes in the bushes. They scanned around greedily until they settled on his sleeping master. Rakush jerked at the rope, but it was tied tightly.

As the dragon came closer and closer, Rakush looked from Rustam to the dragon and back again, sweating with anguish. What should he do? In a few more seconds, his master would certainly be dead. He could bear it no longer. In desperation, he let out a shrill whinny.

Rustam almost jumped out of his skin. "What NOW?" he yelled, but the sight of the hideous dragon right before him silenced him instantly. It lunged for his throat.

Rustam rolled out of the way just in time. Grabbing his sword and shield, he scrambled to his feet.

The dragon glared at him in contempt. Then it opened its mouth and blasted the shield with its fiery breath. In a second, the shield was scorched to cinders.

Seeing the danger his master was in, Rakush reared up with all of his strength. The rope snapped and he leaped to Rustam's aid.

As the dragon turned to face its new enemy, Rustam darted forward, his sword raised. With deadly force, he brought the sword down, slicing right through the dragon's neck. Its head thudded to the ground, and then its body rolled slowly sideways.

Breathing heavily, Rustam turned to Rakush. "It's dead," he said, wiping the sweat from his brow. He reached out to stroke Rakush, but the horse shied away, remembering how his master had scolded him.

"I'm so sorry," said Rustam. "I shouldn't have doubted you. Can you ever forgive me?"

The horse gazed steadily back at his master with his large brown eyes. Then he lowered his head and nuzzled him.

Rustam smiled and stroked Rakush's velvety nose. "What would I do without you, my faithful friend?" he said.

The thirsty dragon

The trees were withered, the lakes lay empty, and dry river beds wound across the land like desert snakes. There wasn't a drop of water anywhere. But it hadn't always been so. Until recently, flowers danced to welcome the morning dew, fish leaped in gurgling streams, and the rain and the sun made rainbows in the sky.

It all began when Indra, the god of thunder, became convinced that a three-headed serpent named Trisiras was preparing to overthrow him. "I can't risk it," thought Indra. "It's him or me." He tracked down Trisiras and waited for the right moment. As he hurled his powerful thunderbolt at the serpent there was a blinding flash. Trisiras didn't stand a chance. The thunderbolt seared through him like a white-hot spear, killing him instantly.

When Trisiras's creator, Tvastri, heard the news of the beast's death, he flew into a rage. "Indra won't get away with this," he seethed. He lit a fire and began to chant under his breath. As he did this, a dragon rose from the flames. It grew and grew until it towered against the sky, blazing like the fiery sun. Flames shot from its mouth and turned the whole sky orange. "I name you Vritra," cried Tvastri. "You will bring about my revenge. Go and destroy Indra."

60

But Vritra had other ideas. The flames had given him a raging thirst and he could think of nothing else. Ignoring his creator, he swung around, looking for something to put out the fire in his throat. In a single sip, he drank a nearby lake dry.

"What are you doing?" cried Tvastri in alarm. Vritra paid no attention. Still burning with thirst, he set off in search of more water. "Come back! Come back at once!" yelled Tvastri, shaking his fists, but he had no power over a monster driven by an unquenchable thirst.

Vritra emptied every river he came to, from dark, underground waterways to crystal-clear mountain streams. Next he moved on to the lakes, and no matter how big they were, he drained every last drop in just one gulp.

When all the lakes were empty too, he ate up the snow on the mountains and licked glaciers and icebergs until not even an icicle was left. Then he reared up on the mountain tops and swallowed the clouds, though they were so light and fluffy that they barely touched his thirst.

Eventually, Vritra reached the sea. The water stretched so far into the distance that he couldn't see where it ended and the sky began. Eagerly, he lowered his head and began to drink. His appearance was so terrifying that the waves turned and sped away from the shore, but his mouth sucked them in like a whirlpool.

Vritra drank and drank until all the water in the seven seas was gone, but the salt made him thirstier than ever. Gasping in desperation, he searched everywhere, but there was no more water to be found. He had drunk the whole world dry.

Feeling weak and exhausted, Vritra curled up in the mountains and settled down to sleep.

When Indra saw what had happened, he knew there was little time to lose. The world couldn't last for long without water. Clutching his thunderbolt, he raced to where Vritra lay sleeping. "Will you give back the waters of the world or must I take them by force?" cried Indra.

With an irritable shudder, Vritra woke up and, by way of an answer, he opened his mouth and swallowed Indra whole.

"Help!" cried Indra as he tumbled helter-skelter down the dragon's throat. The other gods heard his cries and hurried to help, but nothing would persuade Vritra to spit Indra out.

After they had discussed it for some time, one of the gods had an idea. He leaned back casually and pretended to yawn.

As soon as the next god saw this, he couldn't help himself. His eyes scrunched up and his mouth opened wide. Then a third god stretched out his arms and gave a long, sleepy yawn. One after the other, all the gods began to yawn, as if they had caught some mysterious sleeping sickness.

Soon, Vritra's nostrils began to swell too. The gods watched with bated breath as he erupted into the most enormous yawn imaginable.

Down in the dragon's belly, Indra saw his moment. As the light shone into Vritra's open mouth, he made a run for it. He was almost at the end of the tunnel-like throat when Vritra's jaws began to close. In desperation, Indra threw himself at the gap.

He made it through just in time, and the dragon's jaws snapped shut behind him.

Determined not to let Indra escape, Vritra dived after him. As quick as a flash, Indra changed himself into a single hair from a horse's tail, and became all but invisible.

Vritra roared in frustration and a dense fog rushed from his mouth, making it impossible to see.

Indra changed back into his own form and staggered blindly to where he thought Vritra might be. Suddenly, a thunderbolt shot by, narrowly missing him.

"I am the god of thunder — I won't see my own weapons turned against me. Take that!" cried Indra, and he hurled his thunderbolt at Vritra. It sped through the air and struck the immense dragon right in the heart, bringing him crashing to the ground.

Then a strange thing happened. Instead of blood, a tiny fountain of water spurted from the dragon's wound. At first, it was no more than a trickle, but it quickly grew to a raging torrent. As it hit the rocks, it split into separate rivers, which rushed downhill, twisting and turning as each raced to be the first to reach the sea bed.

Indra felt a large raindrop land on his arm, and then another, and another. Suddenly, the heavens opened and the rain flooded down like a vast waterfall. It took Indra's breath away. Closing his eyes, he tilted his face to the sky. The waters of the world had been set free and all was well once more.

65

The big fish

Once there was a poor fisherman. He had been fishing all day, but he hadn't caught a single thing. As the sun sank in the evening sky, he began to haul in his net one last time. To his surprise, it felt heavy. He peered hopefully over the edge of the boat to see what he had caught. There, beneath the waves, a huge shadowy shape was struggling in the net. "What a whopper!" he cried. "I'll have a feast tonight."

Forgetting his tiredness, the fisherman grabbed hold of the ropes and started to pull. He tugged and heaved, and heaved and tugged, until sweat poured down his face, but he couldn't pull the net up. He paused for a moment and took a deep breath. Then, gathering all the strength in his skinny body, he pulled and pulled with all his might. He pulled so hard that the little boat nearly capsized, but the net hardly seemed to move.

The fisherman slumped to his knees and put his head in his hands. "That one fish would be enough to feed everyone in my village for a whole month," he thought to himself. "I can't just let it go." But he realized that, no matter how hard he tried, he'd never be able to haul it in by himself.

"I've got it!" thought the fisherman suddenly. "If I can just get the fish back to the shore, there'll be plenty of people to help me." He tied the net to the back of his boat and, very slowly, he began to row home.

He hadn't gone far when he heard splashing behind him. Glancing back, he saw a flash of golden scales. The big fish was struggling in the net and churning up the water. Worried that his fine catch might escape, the fisherman tried to row faster.

A little later, the fisherman thought he heard a voice. He stopped rowing and listened, but all he could hear was the sound of the waves lapping against the boat. Yet as soon as he started to row, he thought he heard it again. "All this excitement must be getting to me," muttered the fisherman.

Then he heard it absolutely clearly: a rich, silvery voice that sounded as though it came from another world. "Please let me go," it said.

The fisherman looked over his shoulder nervously and his eyes almost popped out of his head. This was no fish; it was a monster! On top of its sleek, scaly body was the fearsome head of a dragon. With a squeal of fright, the fisherman threw himself down in the bottom of the boat and cowered there, trembling.

"Don't be afraid," said the creature softly. "I won't hurt you." Lifting his head doubtfully, the fisherman met its eyes. "I only want to be free," it said.

The fisherman weighed up the situation. It was certainly more than he had bargained for, but this beast didn't sound nearly as scary as it looked, and he was extremely hungry. "It is trapped in the net," he thought to himself. "What harm could it do?"

Feeling a little braver, the fisherman began to row again. Soon, the creature's voice rose above the lapping of the waves once more. "Have a heart," it begged. "I just want to go home."

The fisherman sighed. Somehow, he didn't think his dinner would taste quite the same any more. With a heavy heart and a rumbling tummy, he leaned over the side of the boat and cut the net.

Delighted to be free, the dragon-fish hurled itself into the air, its golden scales gleaming in the light of the setting sun. The fisherman gazed in awe as the majestic creature splashed into the sea.

When it rose to the surface again, the dragon-fish bowed its great head solemnly. "Thank you, my friend," it said. "I am the son of the Dragon King, who rules the sea. I will not forget your kindness."

The fisherman opened his mouth to speak, but before he could find any words the creature had disappeared beneath the waves. "There goes my feast," he sighed, and he began to row home.

The fisherman was still feeling sorry for himself when he went fishing the next morning, but as he caught more and more fish he began to cheer up.

The morning after that, the fisherman's boat had hardly left the shore before the net was full to bursting with fat, shiny fish.

On the third morning, he hadn't even lowered his net into the water when a wet fish landed at his feet. "What on earth?" he exclaimed, as another fish slapped him in the face. It was incredible. The fish were leaping into the boat all by themselves.

The fisherman stared into the water in disbelief and, from fathoms below, in another world, he heard a familiar voice. "I haven't forgotten you," it said.

From that day on, the fisherman never had any trouble catching fish. And whenever he heard fishermen boasting about the size of the fish they had caught, he would just smile to himself and say nothing.

Jack and
the dragaman

Once, there were three brothers named Will, Tom and Jack who lived together in a log cabin, miles away from anywhere. Each day, two of them would go to work in the fields while the third stayed at home to make supper.

One evening, Will was at home alone when he heard something very big and heavy thudding up the path. He flew into a panic. "It must be a bear," he thought, and he scrambled under the table to hide.

He was just out of sight when the door swung open and the most enormous pair of boots he had ever seen stomped right in. When they reached the table, they came to a stop.

There was a pause and then Will heard a loud crunching noise. Nervously, he looked out from under the tablecloth. Hunched over the tiny table was a huge giant. He was chomping through their supper, plates and all. Will shrank back under the table, shaking like a leaf.

When Tom and Jack came back that evening, tired and hungry, they were surprised to find the table empty. "Where's our supper?" asked Tom.

"And what's happened to Will?" added Jack.

When Will heard their voices, he crawled out from under the table. "A g-g-giant ate our s-s-supper," he stammered.

"A g-g-giant?" laughed Tom. "Well I never. Have you been dreaming all afternoon?"

"It's true," said Will indignantly.

The only food left in the house was a little stale bread, so the three brothers all went to bed hungry that night.

The next day, it was Tom's turn to stay at home. "I'll make sure that giant doesn't steal our food again," he chuckled as he waved goodbye to his brothers.

But, later on, when the cups and saucers began to rattle, Tom was no longer chuckling. Not taking any chances, he dived beneath the table.

The giant burst in and marched over to the table. Tom heard his huge lips smacking together loudly as he devoured their supper. Then, when he had eaten every last crumb of food, he stood up, patted his stomach and went on his way.

When Jack and Will returned, they found their supper gone. "Not again!" groaned Jack.

"See! I told you there was a giant," said Will as a pink-faced Tom crawled out from under the table.

"Well, I'll stay here and deal with him tomorrow," said Jack. "I've had enough of going to bed hungry."

The next day, when the giant arrived, Jack was busy laying out their supper. "Come in and help yourself," he called, without even bothering to look up.

The giant peered in through the door suspiciously. He couldn't understand why Jack wasn't afraid. "I don't think so," he said slowly. "I've got some supper waiting for me at home."

"Oh well. Perhaps another time," said Jack cheerily.

"Perhaps..." replied the giant, and he stomped off into the forest. Jack crept after him, taking care to keep hidden among the trees.

Meanwhile, Will and Tom were on their way home. When they got there, they were surprised to find their supper still on the table. "No sign of the giant then, Jack?" said Tom.

There was no reply.

"Jack?" called Will.

Silence.

"The giant must have eaten him!" exclaimed Tom.

"Not likely," said a voice behind them, making them almost jump out of their skins. It was Jack, grinning from ear to ear.

"Where have you been?" asked Will. "Did the giant come?"

"Oh yes," said Jack, "and I thought he was up to something, so I followed him to see where he went." Jack picked up a large basket and a piece of rope. "Come with me," he said.

He led his brothers through the forest until they reached a hole in the ground. "He's down there," said Jack. "I think he's asleep." A rumbling snore from deep underground told them that he was. "Good," said Jack. "Now's our chance. You're the eldest, Will. You go and find out what's going on, and if you want us to pull you up, just tug on the rope."

Will glared at him. He didn't want to look like a coward, so reluctantly he agreed to go. He climbed into the basket and slowly they lowered him into the hole. As he descended, it became darker and darker and the giant's snores grew louder and louder. Will lost his nerve and tugged on the rope.

As quickly as they could, his brothers hauled him up. "What was it? What did you see?" asked Jack.

"Nothing," muttered Will. "How am I supposed to see anything down there without a light?"

"Of course," said Jack, and he hurried home and brought back a candle. Next it was Tom's turn. As they lowered him deeper and deeper into the hole, the flickering candle flame cast strange shadows on the walls, like ghosts and monsters and...giants! Swallowing a scream, Tom yanked on the rope.

74

At once, his brothers heaved him up. "Did you see him?" demanded Jack.

"Not exactly," muttered Tom. "But I'll need something to defend myself with if I do."

"Good idea," said Jack, and he hurried home. "Now it's my turn," he said chirpily as he sauntered back carrying a hatchet. "Wish me luck."

Down and down Jack went, into the darkness. There was a soft thud as the basket reached the bottom. Jack climbed out and held up the candle. He was in a large cave.

Something brushed across his face. Suddenly, he was surrounded by a screeching, flapping mass of bats. As cool as a cucumber, he waited for them to settle, and then began to explore.

He spotted something huddled in the corner of the cave and went to investigate. At the sound of his footsteps, it moved. Jack stopped in his tracks. Gazing up at him was the prettiest girl he had ever seen. "What's a beautiful girl like you doing in a place like this?" he exclaimed.

"Well, what does it look like?" said the girl sharply.

Jack looked down and saw that her hands and feet were tied. "Oh...sorry," he mumbled. "I didn't notice."

"I'm the dragaman's prisoner," she explained.

"Dragaman?" said Jack. "Do you mean the giant?"

"He's not just any old giant," said the girl. "He's a dragon as well, and when he wakes up he's going to eat me."

"Well, there's no need to worry about that now," said Jack confidently. "As sure as my name's Jack, I'll have you out of here in a jiffy." Deftly, he untied the knots and helped her to her feet. "Let's go," he said.

As they turned to leave, the ground began to shake and pieces of rock fell from the roof of the cave. Some very heavy footsteps were coming their way. "Quick, hide," said Jack, pushing the girl behind a rock.

"What are YOU doing here?" boomed the giant when he saw Jack.

"I'm here to set your prisoner free," replied Jack bravely.

"How dare you!" bellowed the giant. Then, to Jack's horror, he dropped onto all fours and began to growl. His teeth grew to long, sharp points and scales burst through his hairy skin. "Don't mess with the dragaman," he roared, and spat out a huge fireball.

A whole volley of fireballs followed close behind. Jack dodged this way and that, but they came so thick and fast that, nimble as he was, he could hardly get out of their way.

"Get him, Jack!" urged the girl.

Her words distracted Jack just for a moment and one of the fireballs caught him on the shoulder. He let out a cry of pain and dropped the hatchet.

The dragon turned and saw the girl crouching behind the rock. He bared his teeth at her.

"Leave her alone!" shouted Jack, and he ran at the dragon. When he was close enough, he took a swipe at him. The hatchet's blade struck the dragon's neck, but barely left a scratch.

Undaunted, Jack whirled the hatchet around his head until it was a blur of silver. Then he struck again. This time, it sliced clean through the dragon's neck, sending the creature's head tumbling to the ground.

"Let's get out of here," cried Jack. He led the girl back through the cave to where the basket was dangling. Then he helped her into it and tugged on the rope.

"Will you do something for me?" Jack called out as the basket swung up towards the light.

"What?" she answered.

"Marry me!" he cried.

Jack could no longer see the girl's face, but his heart leaped as her answer echoed back a thousand times over: "Yes...yes...yes...yes...yes..."

When the girl reached the top, Will let out a gasp.

"Hey! I saw her first," said Tom.

Each of the brothers grabbed one of her arms to help her out of the basket. "Let go," said Will, giving Tom a shove.

"No way," retorted Tom. They pulled the poor girl back and forth until she thought she would split in two.

"Stop it!" she shouted. "I've already promised to marry Jack."

The two brothers stopped. "Oh," they said, feeling foolish.

"So, you see, it's no use squabbling," she continued. "Now come and help me to pull him out."

Together, the three of them pulled on the rope, and soon Jack's beaming face appeared. He jumped from the basket and swung his bride-to-be in circles until they were dizzy with happiness.

Will and Tom watched enviously, but even they had to smile in the end. "Let's live happily ever after," said Jack. And that's just what they did.

The dancing dragon

Once upon a time, high in the mountains, there lived a woman and her daughter. The girl was known as Little Red because she loved to dress all in red.

One day, as Little Red and her mother were working in the rice fields together, a gale blew up suddenly. They stopped what they were doing and looked up at the sky, puzzled by the change in the weather. In the distance, they saw a large dark cloud, which seemed to be coming their way.

"I think we'd better go inside," said Little Red's mother. They hurried across the fields, but the wind swirled around them, pushing them back.

As the sky grew darker, Little Red's mother glanced up again. The cloud was right overhead. She screamed, for hidden inside the cloud was a huge storm dragon. It swooped down and snatched up Little Red in its powerful claws.

Little Red's mother tried to grab hold of her daughter's feet, but they swung out of reach. "Don't worry," called Little Red bravely. "I'll be back."

81

But Little Red's mother
was very worried indeed.
Barely able to see through her
tears, she staggered home,
weeping for the loss of her
only child. She was so
distracted that she wasn't
watching where she was
going and found herself
caught up in the branches
of a bayberry tree.

As she struggled to
free herself, some of the
berries came off in her hand.
They were as round and red
as could be. She popped them into her mouth. Much to her
surprise, the branches opened immediately and she was able
to continue on her way.

The same night, an incredible thing happened. Without
any warning at all, Little Red's mother gave birth to a baby
boy. He had a round, smiling face and cheeks as red as berries,
so she called him Bayberry.

Bayberry grew amazingly quickly. By the next morning,
he came up to his mother's waist; the following morning,
he was almost up to her shoulder; and by the third morning,
he had grown into a fine young man.

That afternoon, Bayberry was sitting under a tree when he overheard two crows talking to one another. "Poor Little Red," said one.

"Yes, poor Little Red," agreed the other. "It's such a shame that Bayberry isn't brave enough to rescue his own sister."

Bayberry jumped up. "What do you mean?" he asked. "I don't even have a sister."

"Did you hear that?" said the first crow. "He said he doesn't have a sister."

"Shocking," said the second crow, shaking its head in disgust. "I think we've heard enough, don't you?" And, with that, they flew up into the sky.

Bayberry stared after them in total bewilderment. Then he went inside and told his mother what he had heard.

Her eyes filled with tears. "It's true. You do have a sister," she sobbed, and she told him how the dragon had carried Little Red away.

Bayberry listened thoughtfully. "The birds are right. I must rescue her," he said when his mother had finished.

"Please don't go," his mother begged. "I've already lost one child. I couldn't bear to lose another." But she knew in her heart that he had to leave.

Bayberry cut down a branch and stripped it to make a walking stick. Then he said goodbye and set off into the mountains in search of his sister. He had been walking for many miles when he came across a boulder blocking his path.

Bayberry tried to lever it out of the way with his stick, but the stick snapped in two. So he bent down and, gripping the rock with both hands, heaved as hard as he could. Slowly, the rock began to shift, and a moment later it crashed down the mountainside into the valley below.

Lying on the path where the rock had been was a little golden reed pipe. Bayberry picked it up and blew it. A single, sweet note rang out and a lizard shot from under a stone. Bayberry played a little tune and two more lizards appeared. The three of them stood in a line, lifting up their feet in time to the music. Then a frog and a rabbit hopped over to join them, and an earthworm popped up and began to sway.

The faster Bayberry played, the faster the animals danced. They just couldn't help themselves. By the time he laid his pipe down, the earthworm had tied itself up in knots. Gently, Bayberry untied the little creature. Then he tucked the golden pipe into his pocket and went on his way.

After a few more miles, Bayberry came to the foot of a steep, rocky peak. It looked like just the sort of place where a dragon might choose to live, so he began to climb it. Sure enough, as he climbed higher, he saw a mean-looking dragon pacing up and down in front of the entrance to a cave. He hid himself behind a rock and watched.

"Hurry up, you useless girl," moaned the dragon. "You'll never finish my lovely new cave at this rate."

Bayberry peered around the rock to see who the dragon was talking to. He saw a pretty, young girl dressed all in red chipping away at the rock with a pick. Immediately, Bayberry guessed that this was his sister.

"Faster," said the dragon, lashing out at her with its tail.

It was more than Bayberry could bear. "Stop it!" he shouted, rushing out from his hiding place.

"And who do you think you are?" sneered the dragon.

"My name is Bayberry and this is my sister, Little Red," said Bayberry. "I've come to rescue her."

"Oh really?" said the dragon. "How very charming." It took a step in Bayberry's direction, expecting him to run away, but Bayberry simply took out the golden pipe and began to play.

At once, the dragon's feet began to tap. It looked down at them suspiciously. "What the—?" it began. But, before it could figure out what was going on, its head was flicking and its feet were kicking in time to the music.

Faster and faster Bayberry played, and faster and faster the dragon danced. Then it started to spin. It whirled so fast that it was almost a blur. Its tail whistled as it whipped around and steam shot from its nostrils. "Stop!" it gasped.

But Bayberry didn't stop. He began to skip down the mountainside, and the dragon had no choice but to follow. It bounded after him, leaping through the air like a clumsy goat. Little Red could barely keep up with them.

Eventually, Bayberry reached a lake. Still playing, he climbed onto a large rock. Then he watched as the dragon hopped and skipped right down to the water, where it landed with a huge splash.

Bayberry was drenched from head to toe, but he didn't stop playing, not even for a moment. And the dragon didn't stop dancing either. It splashed around in time to the music, doing dragon-paddle to stay afloat.

After a while, the dragon became very tired indeed. "Please stop," it glugged, swallowing a huge mouthful of water. "I promise I won't hurt you or your sister."

Bayberry raised an eyebrow. He wasn't sure whether to believe the dragon or not.

"Please," it begged. "I'll do anything you ask."

It sounded so miserable and desperate that Bayberry gave in and lowered his pipe.

The second the music stopped, the dragon stopped dancing too. It grinned maliciously, and splashed over to where Bayberry and Little Red were standing. "Fool!" it screeched, as soon as it was on dry land. "Did you really think that I'd keep my promise?"

Bayberry didn't even bother to reply. He just put his pipe to his lips and began to play. To the dragon's horror, it lurched into another dance. "I'm sorry," it cried. "I was only joking."

But this time Bayberry didn't stop, no matter how much the dragon begged. He wasn't going to fall for that trick again. Faster and faster he trilled, and the dragon squirmed and writhed in the wildest dance you could possibly imagine.

Bayberry played on and on, into the night. Showers of shooting stars burst from the heavens and the moon led a midnight dance across the sky. Then, when morning came, the birds flew down and joined him in a dawn chorus.

For seven days and seven nights Bayberry played. Each day, the dragon grew weaker, but no matter how much it wanted to, it just couldn't stop dancing. Finally, the day came when the dragon could dance no more, and it sank to the bottom of the lake for good.

Mysterious Melusine

Melusine was sitting in a forest glade beside the fairy fountain when a handsome young man rode up to her. She captured his heart instantly. "You're the most beautiful woman I've ever seen," he exclaimed impulsively. "Will you marry me?"

Melusine laughed, a pretty, tinkling laugh. "You haven't even told me your name yet," she said.

The young man flushed. "I'm terribly sorry," he said, climbing down from his horse. "You must think me very rude. My name is Raymond."

"Well, Raymond, this is all rather sudden," said Melusine. "Perhaps I will marry you, but there's something you must promise me first."

"Anything at all," he replied. "What is it?"

"You mustn't tell anyone where you met me and you must never see me on a Saturday," she said.

Raymond smiled. These were rather strange requests, but they seemed harmless enough. "As you wish," he said.

"Then let's be married," said Melusine, and together they galloped away through the trees.

A week later, Raymond and Melusine were married. Afterwards, there was a magnificent feast, with hundreds of guests, all eager to meet Raymond's mysterious bride.

89

"You dark horse," said Raymond's uncle, nudging him and winking. "I've never seen her before. Who is she and where is she from?"

"She's my own true love," said Raymond, and then he quickly changed the subject.

Melusine, meanwhile, charmed everyone she spoke to with her wit and beauty. Only Raymond's brother hung back, with a suspicious look on his face. But Raymond and Melusine were so happy that they didn't even notice.

When, at last, the final guests departed, Melusine thanked Raymond for keeping his promise. "If you will always do so, we will live happily together and fortune will smile on us," she said.

The next morning, on the very spot where they had made their wedding vows, a beautiful castle appeared. When Melusine showed it to Raymond, he was absolutely astounded. "But...how? I don't understand..." he whispered.

"What is there to understand?" said Melusine softly. "You just need to trust me."

So Raymond did. They became more and more wealthy and their land grew and grew, but that wasn't all. During the night, fortresses, churches, towers and sometimes entire towns would magically appear. Raymond was delighted at his sudden good fortune, and hardly dared to question it.

Every Saturday, Melusine would lock herself away in one of the castle's towers until the following morning. Raymond burned with curiosity, but he kept his promise and left her alone.

The months flew by, and Melusine gave birth to their first child. It was a baby boy. When Raymond picked him up, he saw that the baby had one red eye and one blue eye. "What incredible eyes!" he remarked to Melusine, and they were both as proud of their son as could be.

A year later, Melusine gave birth to their second son. Once again, Raymond was overjoyed, but as he bent down to kiss the baby, he noticed that one of his ears was much, much bigger than the other. "All the better to hear with," Raymond laughed, and tickled the enormous ear.

As their family grew, each child was unusual in some way. One had only one eye, while another had three; another child had one enormous tooth and yet another had a tuft of hair sprouting from the end of his nose. There was even a child with a lion's paw growing from his cheek. But Raymond loved them dearly and didn't mind their strange appearance at all.

Raymond and Melusine lived happily together, and their love continued to grow. Then, one day, everything changed. It was a Saturday and Melusine had gone off to the tower as usual. Raymond's brother arrived unexpectedly. He chatted for a while to Raymond and then asked after Melusine.

"I'm afraid she's not here," said Raymond lightly.

"I see," said his brother, with a frown.

"Is something wrong?" asked Raymond.

His brother looked embarrassed. "It's just that people are starting to talk," he said. "The way Melusine disappears every Saturday – they say she must have some dark secret."

"What nonsense!" said Raymond. But, after his brother had left, his words began to play on Raymond's mind. In the end, his curiosity got the better of him. He went to the tower where Melusine spent every Saturday and crept up the stairs. At the top, there was a solid wooden door. Raymond bent down and peered through the keyhole. He could just see Melusine sitting in a bathtub. He staggered back with a cry of horror. From the waist down, his beautiful wife had turned into a dragon.

Melusine heard the noise and hurried to the door. Raymond was still standing there, too shocked to move. He stared down at her clawed feet and long scaly tail.

"You promised never to look," she said accusingly.

"I know," said Raymond. "I couldn't help it."

Melusine shook her head sadly. "I am under a spell," she explained. "If you had trusted me, we could have been happy, but now you know my dark secret I must live as a dragon until the end of my days."

As Melusine turned to go, Raymond grabbed her arm. "It's too late," she said, pushing him away. At that moment, her fingers curled into sharp claws. She looked at them in horror and with a desperate sob she rushed outside.

"Wait," called Raymond, running out after her. She turned to face him, her eyes glistening with tears. The scales had already crept right up to her neck. The Melusine he knew was almost gone.

"You should have trusted me," she said, and she threw herself from the tower. As Melusine fell, leathery wings sprouted from her shoulders and caught the air. She let out a wail, which grew louder and louder until it became a deafening screech. Three times she circled the tower; then she flew away over the hills.

Every now and again, Melusine would fly back in the middle of the night to see their children, but poor Raymond never, ever saw her again.

With thanks to the following for advice about the stories:
Dr. Trevor Bryce, University of Queensland,
Dr. Arshia Sattar and Dr. Abigail Wheatley.

First published in 2006 by Usborne Publishing Ltd,
Usborne House, 83-85 Saffron Hill, London EC1N 8RT, England.
www.usborne.com Copyright © 2006 Usborne Publishing Ltd.
The name Usborne and the devices ♀ ⊕ are Trade Marks of Usborne Publishing Ltd.
First published in America in 2007. U.E. Printed in Dubai.